ACHILLES' HEEL

By The Same Author

The Myth of June

Asclepius' Descent: A Plague Chronicles Short

The Oath of Eve

Achilles' Heel: A Plague Chronicles Short

The Wrath of Raine

Non-Fiction Pen Name

Then I Was Taken by Alaina Davis

Achilles' Heel

A Plague Chronicles Short

A. B. Daniels-Annachi

First published in The United States
This edition 1

Pacific Publications
P.O. Box 1366 Corvallis OR 97333

Copyright © 2022 A. B. Daniels-Annachi
Internal design © Pacific Publications/Etheric Designs
Cover design & Artwork © Art Lynx Covers
Typeset by ProDesign, Etheric
Edited by Lauren Donovan – Book Foundry Editing

All rights reserved. No part of this book may
be reproduced in any form or by any electronic
or mechanical means including photocopying,
recording, storage in an information retrieval
system, or otherwise – except in the case of brief
quotations embodied in critical articles or reviews
– without permission in writing from its publisher,
Pacific Publications.

The book is a work of fiction. Names, characters,
places, and incidents are either a product of the
author's imagination or are used fictitiously. Any
similarity to real persons, living or dead, business
establishments, events, or locales is coincidental
and not intended by the author.

Any brand or product names used in this book are
trademarks of their respective holders and are not
associated with Pacific Publications.

ISBN 978 1 922936 57 8

Potential Triggers: Alcoholism, Bullying, Car Accident, Death, Explicit Descriptions of Illness/Injury, Suicidal Ideation

A character may be thrown into anguish when they find out that they are only a passerby in another's story. That any person might have their own ambitions and worries, or even prophecies to fulfill, as each of their lives sprawl through endless potential timelines, could be world-shattering.

To understand the Olympians' pasts fully, their stories must be consumed in pieces. This short will change the story, depending where in The Plague Chronicles it is read. The author recommends that "Achilles' Heel" be read after "The Oath of Eve."

ACHILLES

The hair on the back of Achilles' neck stood on end as he drove. Something felt wrong, but he wasn't sure what, exactly. A sense of impending doom shuddered up his spine, and his heart thudded hard in his chest. He glanced into the rearview mirror, as if he might find someone following him, but when he saw that the road was empty, he chastised himself and tried to ignore the feeling of unease. As he turned the steering wheel around the curves of the road that led home, his husband reached across the seat and placed a hand on his thigh.

"Are you okay?" Patroclus asked with a wrinkle in his brow.

Achilles nodded, squaring his shoulders. He turned into their driveway and yanked the gearshift into park, offering him a smile.

"I'm great," he lied.

His gaze caught on the sun-colored curl that flopped over Patroclus' forehead, before landing on his eyes.

"What are you looking at?" Patroclus asked, swatting his chest.

Achilles leaned in and kissed his cheek before popping the latch on his door. "Just committing you to memory so that when I die," he said with a wink, "I will carry you with me to Elysium."

He heard Patroclus chuckle as he rounded the car and opened his door. He bowed low and flourished his arm. Patroclus' eyes crinkled with his grin as he stepped out of his seat and picked up the box of groceries, and Achilles enjoyed the warmth that spread through his chest.

He was so busy watching Patroclus' fluid movements that he nearly tripped over the bundle of mail sitting in front of the step. He bent to pick it up and frowned at a thick brown envelope beneath their normal bills.

"Honey, are you expecting anything?" Achilles called into the kitchen.

"Not aside from the mortgage."

Achilles' brow furrowed at the abnormal piece of mail. The return address was unfamiliar, there were too many stamps in the right corner, and it was heavy. He flipped it over and touched the multiple layers of tape sealing the flap shut.

"There's something big in here, is all. Don't worry, I got it." He let his voice fade as the sound of rustling butcher's paper filled the air.

Achilles shook his head and walked into their living room, setting the pile of letters on a small wooden table near his favorite armchair. He yanked open the heavy curtain that blocked the window facing the street. A stream of sunlight flooded the room, illuminating the space and throwing rainbows against the sage green walls between paintings. He fluffed the pillow in Patroclus' armchair before sliding into his house slippers and watching a neighbor pull into a driveway across the street.

Patroclus began humming, so Achilles picked up the big envelope once again and strode to the kitchen island, plucking a knife from a drawer before sitting and swiping it open.

He pulled the packet out and began to read the letter. By the time he made it to the end, his fingers were trembling. He started over again, gripping the edges and pulling the sheet taut, nearly to the point of tearing. He devoured the words, scanning the top page again and again.

He vaguely heard Patroclus move around in front of him, and questions pushed against his eardrums, but the blood rushing through his skull drowned them out.

His eyes swam with tears, and the black ink on the page bled together until he couldn't make out the individual letter strokes. He leaned back in his seat and let his arm fall, looking to the ceiling as he cried. Heavy, hard sobs wailed from his chest.

Patroclus grabbed his head and looked between his eyes. "What is it? What does it say?" his husband demanded.

Achilles tried to find the words, but anguish gripped his heart like a vice, and as he opened his mouth, his sobs renewed. Patroclus rubbed a pattern between the muscles in his back and murmured reassurance.

It took a few more minutes for Achilles to settle himself enough that he could pull away and clear his throat, sniffling. He wiped his nose and exhaled, and Patroclus kissed his forehead.

Achilles took a last breath before he lifted the letter with both hands and began to read aloud. "Thetis, Achilles."

Patroclus' honey eyes met Achilles' teal ones before they both looked back down, and Achilles continued reading. "You are ordered to the location shown below for training, to transfer for active duty—" Patroclus choked and raised a trembling hand to his lips, but Achilles continued through a wavering voice. "For a period up to ten years, unless sooner released or extended..." Achilles' voice trailed off, and he lowered the sheet. "It continues with deployment details and a copy of a service contract."

Patroclus shook his head slowly, tears brimming in his eyes, as he whispered the word 'No.' He backed away a step and tripped backward, still clutching at Achilles.

Achilles let the paper fall to the ground and wrapped his arms around his husband, who returned the embrace. "I never thought this would happen." His throat was raw, and his voice came out hoarse.

"Will you even come back from this?" Patroclus asked and curled into his embrace harder.

Achilles' mind began racing as he pondered the implications of the notice; he owed the Fates his life, on behalf of his mother. He'd avoided it for the last thirty years of his life, but he couldn't see a way to skirt death for a ten-year deployment.

He glanced down to the letter at his feet and scanned the page for his service location but couldn't make out any details through the blur of his tears. He looked up at the pink splotches blooming across Patroclus' cheeks and offered him a weak smile.

"I'm practically a god, remember? I'll come back," Achilles joked, but a sinking feeling settled deep in the pit of his stomach.

"Do you think this is it? That Thetis' prophecy is coming around?" Patroclus' voice was steeped in worry, and it sent a pang of pain through Achilles' chest.

He said nothing as he held his husband and listened to his heart race. He wanted desperately to offer more comforting words, but they all evaded him.

Every choice he'd made, from the moment he learned to walk, was meant to lead to his becoming a great warrior. He would bring fame and honor to his mother's name, to Thetis, by dying a hero. That was the future told before his birth.

Granted, she had tried to curb the death aspect of his fate by birthing him in The River Styx, but he held no faith that the Fates would allow him to escape the future that was woven into the thread of his life. He had told Patroclus as much when they met.

He looked up. His gaze wandered over Patroclus' high cheekbones, his sharp jaw, the light stubble grazing it, and back up to his bright burst of lashes framing his golden eyes, which brimmed with tears. He may not have the words, but he would remember every moment they had left, at least. Just as he'd vowed when they married.

"We can conquer anything that comes our way, together," Patroclus said in a small voice.

Achilles stood and gathered him in his arms, pressing his lips against Patroclus', before moving up, kissing away the droplets that had begun to fall.

"I don't know if this is it. It might be, but you're right, we can conquer anything. The war that has been brewing has to end soon. There's no way it will truly last another ten years," Achilles said.

Patroclus' back bowed with invisible weight as he took a deep breath and nodded. "What if I go with you?" he whispered.

Achilles' head snapped back, and an anxious heat crept up his neck. "Absolutely not. You're not risking your life to follow me into battle. It's insane enough that I'm expected to go."

Patroclus pulled away and settled into the chair next to him, rubbing circles on his arm and nodding. "I thought the draft was a myth, honestly. Is there a process to select who gets chosen, or is it random?"

Achilles shrugged. "I knew they might conscript civilians for the war when it came here, but I didn't consider how that might impact us."

How had he let this time creep up so quickly? He should have prepared better. They should have planned for this. He should have been ready for his fate. Maybe he could have gone and bargained with the Fates at some point before.

He set his head in his hand, watching a patch of sunlight move from one end of the counter to the other before a touch on his shoulder made him jump. He turned back around to face Patroclus, and a few more cars pulling into neighboring driveways caught his eye. His brows knit together.

As if reading his mind, his husband cleared his throat. "Do you think we should check in with the Johnsons? They have those four children, and I know Howard served in the military."

Achilles shook his head. "No, I'm sure it was a fluke." He scrubbed his face. "There's no way it's true, I'm not getting deployed."

Patroclus smiled warmly. "We could pretend the letter didn't even come. There was nothing left on the doorstep."

Achilles laughed. "No one lives here!"

Patroclus chuckled, and before his smile faded, he reached a hand over the counter. "Remember when we were young, and we used to play war in the schoolyard?"

Achilles swallowed hard, his gaze settling on his husband. He nodded. "I'd told you about my future."

"You were so set on fulfilling the prophecy then. You wanted that destined greatness that Thetis told you of."

"I was also a child and had no concept of what was for lunch the next day, let alone the concept of war or growing up, Patroclus."

"We spent so many days slaying our enemies and fighting for justice," Patroclus said, turning his eyes down. "I also wanted to die a hero, at that point. What changed?"

"I hadn't fallen in love with you yet," he whispered and turned Patroclus' hand over and held it. "I couldn't enlist and leave you after that."

"The gods really have created an awful predicament," Patroclus pondered.

Achilles squeezed his fingers. "I want to have faith, but I'm worried that this is it, Pat."

Patroclus lifted his head from Achilles' shoulder and looked him in the eye. "In the twenty years that we've been friends, I've never known you to be a quitter."

"But the Fates—"

"But nothing," Patroclus interrupted him. "I'm not losing my husband after it took him so long to marry me." A small smile pulled the corner of his mouth up, and Achilles leaned in and kissed him before the frown could show on his own.

It was great that Patroclus imagined that they could escape the future together, but the other potential path began to play itself out in Achilles' mind.

Patroclus stood, and Achilles moved to do the same, but the anxious feeling crashed over him again.

"I'm scared," he muttered, leaning against the table.

"Achilles..."

Patroclus reached out, but Achilles was already walking toward the door.

"I'm going out. I need to think."

His vision blurred as the door slammed behind him, and a small part of his mind called out that it wasn't fair to Pat for him to leave. He quickly smothered it and tried to steady his breathing as he sat in the car.

Patroclus could feel fine about the prophecy and deployment all he wanted, and they could ignore the letter, sure.

But Achilles had never told Patroclus the rest of the prophecy. He didn't understand it when he was small, and as he matured, he wondered if sharing the rest might chase his partner away. So, he'd kept it tucked away, and occasionally only thought briefly of the fact that no matter what, his fate was chosen for him.

He could choose to become, and die, a hero.

But Thetis had angered the Fates when she birthed him in the Styx, in the river of oaths, in her attempt to barter with them. The Fates had issued an amendment to his prophecy. He wouldn't just die a hero if he entered battle. If he tried to avoid his fate, tried to live a quiet life, death would chase him; no matter what, he would die young.

He felt as if he couldn't breathe as he jerked the car into gear. He swerved around the bend in the road, narrowly avoiding a driver heading the other direction. His heart raced as he drove, his foot pressing harder into the gas pedal as the back of his throat grew more raw and his nose leaked.

By the time he reached a parking lot where he felt safe to pull over, the tears were pricking his eyes painfully again. He gripped the wheel with both hands and screamed at the dash before slamming his palm against the horn twice.

"Why?" he yelled. The sliver of voice that escaped him was hoarse, and the cool metal of the car's emblem bit into his skin as he leaned to rest his forehead against the center of the wheel.

Why what? Why was he getting deployed, or why must he have a preordained fate? He was unsure if he was asking himself the question, or the gods. Perhaps he wasn't even asking a question that needed an answer.

Achilles took a deep breath and prepared to sit up again, but a rap on the window startled him. His head snapped up, and he turned to find a beautiful, grinning face pressed against his window. He glanced around, but no other vehicles were in the lot, and when he looked back, the unease winding through his shoulders loosened slightly.

"Hi, stranger." The man waved a slender hand, and his breath fogged up the glass.

A sudden wave of comfort enveloped Achilles. He felt like he knew this man. He relaxed and swung the door open to look his visitor up and down.

His piercing blue eyes were fixed on Achilles, and Achilles' own bounced between the perfect angles of his face and the carved muscles of his arms. The man's long fingers pushed a curtain of thick ringlets from his face, and he smiled with unnaturally white teeth. Everything about him was too perfect. A god could have carved this man from marble and Achilles still wouldn't be convinced he existed.

"Are you okay?" he asked.

A beat passed between them before he cleared his throat, and Achilles looked into his eyes again.

"Right. Yes, I am," Achilles said.

No, he wasn't.

"You were having quite a fit." The man nodded to the building Achilles had parked in front of, and he noticed a neon sign in the shape of a spilled wine glass for the first time. One of the walnut-colored double doors was propped open, and music leaked into the night air.

"Care to have a drink and talk about it?"

Achilles shook his head and tightened his grip on the door handle, vaguely wondering why he was still sitting in his car. "I can't—don't—drink. I should get home, actually."

"Have a glass of wine with me, you might feel better." The man's grin widened, causing his eyes to narrow, and Achilles paused.

He had left to think and get some space; maybe a drink would clear his mind. It had been a long time. Surely he could handle just one. He didn't see a reason not to.

"Alright, yeah." Achilles slammed the car door shut and followed the man to the entrance tucked under the pink sign.

It took a moment for his vision to adjust. The bar was dim, more so than it probably needed to be. A lineup of tables and whiskey barrel seats were pushed against a heavily postered wall. A round bar in the middle of the room was surrounded by metal stools. Achilles looked around as he slid onto an empty seat and realized that there was no one else in the bar. The only sound filling the room was music, which he couldn't place the source of.

"Hey..." he trailed off as he also remembered that he didn't know the man's name.

"You can call me Dio." Dio's voice came from directly over Achilles' shoulder and startled him.

He chuckled nervously and scratched his chin. Dio walked around him and jumped onto the bar, swinging a leg over before dropping to the other side.

"What're you doing?" he asked.

Dio winked as he produced two wine glasses from beneath the counter with a flourish. "Serving us drinks, of course. This is my bar."

"Oh, I didn't know." Achilles rubbed his hands together before reaching for his wallet.

"Don't worry about it, first glass is on me. You clearly need the conversation, and libation," he said in a joking tone and raised his glass.

Achilles cleared his throat and lifted his drink to his lips. "Thank you, Dio." He took a long draw of the sweet red and closed his eyes as the notes of fruit danced across his tongue.

"So, what brings you crying to my parking lot tonight?"

Achilles set his glass down and spun the stem in a circle with a nervous laugh. "That is a loaded question."

Dio spread his arms wide. "It looks like we have time, unless someone else stumbles in here."

Achilles took another drink and waited until the warmth had spread through his chest before speaking.

"I'm married."

Dio raised a brow. "Congratulations. So is half the population."

The corner of Achilles' mouth lifted. "That's not why—well, partially it is." He met Dio's intense gaze and leaned on his hand. "I love my husband more than anything— More than my own life. We've known each other since we were eight."

Dio nodded. "I was in love once."

Achilles drank again and continued. "I was told I had to join the military. I didn't though, for him. And myself, but for him, you know? Now I have no choice, I've been drafted, and I know I won't return from service."

Dio refilled their glasses before setting a fresh bottle on the bar and climbing back over to sit on the stool next to Achilles. He crossed an ankle over his leg and raised a brow.

"Why can't you just say no?" he asked.

"It's complicated." Achilles sighed and drained his second glass. He looked to the ceiling and took a breath as the buzz spread through his body. "It's ten years."

Dio nodded somberly and stood. He walked around the bar, and Achilles kept his gaze trained on him. He realized, as the bartender walked, that Dio was only wearing loose linen pants and an unbuttoned shirt. His feet were bare, and though he'd walked outside, they appeared to be unmarred from the gravel lot.

"Do you believe in fate, Achilles?" Dio asked.

Achilles looked back up at him as he opened the refrigerator and nodded. The music floating through the air garbled in his ears, and his vision blurred. He leaned on the counter and looked down.

Dio was pouring another round for them, and a loud ding filled the air when he cashed in the till. Achilles raised a brow but said nothing, only sipping from his drink. He felt in his pocket and wondered where his wallet had gone before Dio handed it back to him.

He looked over at his drinking buddy then, and a laugh bubbled in his throat.

"Were you ever wearing shoes?"

Dio chuckled. "You didn't answer my question, but I suppose that answer could be subjective. Are you referring to the 'ever' since you met me, or 'ever' in the general sense of life? Or just today."

Achilles shook his head, confused, but Dio continued speaking.

"I wonder if you didn't end up at my bar for a reason. I stood in your place once." Dio tapped the edge of his glass, and Achilles cocked his head. The glass was full, but he could have sworn that a moment earlier it had been nearly empty, and neither of them had moved.

"There was a time in my life where I felt I was up against an impossible enemy. The Fates had it out for me—"

"That's it!" Achilles interrupted him. "It's the Fates! My mother and that damned prophecy." He trailed off and mumbled a few words, unsure if he should say anything else.

Dio grinned and snapped. "Yes, exactly. To this day I'm unsure if the Fates truly interfered in my life, but I would believe it. Years ago, I was thrown into a fight against a man who, ironically, was in the military. He brought his whole force against me and mine, and I was forced to flee and give up a good portion of my life and what I valued."

Achilles watched his mouth as he spoke, hanging on to every word. There was something in the back of his mind that told him there were details missing from the story, but he couldn't place what exactly was wrong as Dio's thick pink lips formed the words about his struggle. He nodded along as Dio spoke about fleeing the land that was his home.

"I sought refuge with my friend in the sea. She kept me safe until the situation resolved itself, but it felt as if I was up against an impossible choice for a long time. I had to—"

Achilles straightened. "In the sea?" he interrupted to ask. His mind felt slow as he realized what Dio had said. "What do you mean 'in'?"

Dio waved his hand. "Near, in, it's all the same." He raised his glass, and Achilles mimicked him, nodding. Surely it was. His mother lived in the sea.

"Exactly, Thetis." Dio shrugged. "She's Nereid."

Achilles rose from his seat, shocked. Was Dio in his mind? Had he said that aloud? "That's my mother," he muttered.

Dio braced a hand on his shoulder and helped him sit again. "That couldn't be more obvious. You look just like her, and reek of sea water."

Achilles frowned and narrowed his eyes at Dio. "I do not. My husband thinks I smell quite good, thank you very much." He looked over Dio again, as his mind raced, and his vision blurred. He was quite sure that he'd only thought the words about his mother and not said them out loud. Dio's grin widened, and Achilles' jaw dropped. "You're a god, aren't you?"

Dio winked. "A demigod, technically. Twice born might make me a full god, depending who you ask." He lifted his glass toward Achilles before taking a long drink, and Achilles blinked as the glass was set down, completely full, again. "Anyway, my point was that sometimes it feels as if you only have one direction but really there is a way to escape. I thought I would die by that attack, but I found refuge with Thetis. She knew best."

Achilles refocused on Dio, and his words stumbled over each other. "But she's the reason I'm in this mess. She has no way to relieve me of it." He took a deep breath and launched into the explanation of his prophecy and the choice that he was up against. He ended with the fact that he was leaving behind Patroclus no matter which route he took.

"It sounds like you're between a rock and a hard place," Dio said. He scratched the stubble on his cheek and threw his curls back over his shoulder. "Have you considered just asking the Fates to rescind their ruling?"

Achilles blanched. "I don't think they would do that. This was set out long before my time. Not to mention, mom tried to find a way out. With the Styx."

"Oh, yeah."

Achilles tried to roll his eyes but became dizzy from the move. He grabbed the edge of the bar to steady himself and looked down to see five empty wine bottles between them. He sunk back into his seat and set his head on the counter.

"I just wish the prophecy had never been set. Why do I have to be surprised by death either way? No matter which way I go, I don't know when it'll come, but I'll be running."

He felt a firm hand on his shoulder. "Maybe that's your way out. Take your death into your own hands. Greet it before it takes you."

Achilles closed his eyes and nodded. The buzz flowed through his mind and down his spine, and he embraced the warmth from the wine that filled his belly for a few moments. He could greet death now.

Light flickered behind his eyelids, and he felt a shroud begin to fall around the edges of his mind. He sat up quickly as a realization struck him.

"You're Dionysus!" he exclaimed.

But he was alone in his car, and the seat next to him was empty. He raised a hand to his forehead and felt the slight depression from the emblem on the steering wheel. He popped the door handle and could have sworn that the window had the slightest bit of condensation from someone's breath on it, but no one was outside. The neon sign he thought had been lit up earlier was gone. There was no hint of music in his ears.

He climbed back into his car and tried to shake the fog from his mind. The drive home was short, but he took it very carefully. He wasn't sure how long he'd been gone, and he knew that Patroclus would be worried.

Every turn on the drive home sent his mind winding back through his conversation with Dio. Had it truly occurred, or was it all in his head? Was there a way for him to take his fate into his own hands?

The curves in the road blurred, and he pulled the wheel hard to the right as the pavement wove around a hill. The fog line rumbled under the tires, the wheel trembled, and he jerked the car to the left.

He recentered in the lane with a gasp. He'd come too close to grating the car against the metal bumper. A car crash was not how he wanted to try and go, and even though he thought he would make it out just fine, the mass of metal he drove would not; Patroclus would have his head for damaging it.

Achilles took a deep breath and slowed for the rest of the drive, pulling into his driveway at a snail's pace. He killed the engine and turned off the headlights before peering up at the dark house. The rooms behind the windows were still; Patroclus had gone to bed.

Achilles crept through the living room quietly, avoiding the creaky floorboard in front of the stairs before ascending. He grimaced at the clock that had never had a replacement battery put into it. He had no idea what time it was and couldn't be sure if he should be upset that Patroclus didn't wait up for him.

He gripped the handrail as if it were a rope he was using to scale a mountain as he climbed the steps one at a time. The sound of Patroclus' rhythmic breathing filled the air as Achilles froze in the doorway and leaned against the frame.

How was his husband sleeping so soundly?

Achilles expected that he would have been worried sick, maybe pacing the floors. Or at least awake in bed and waiting for him to wander in. His mind raced as he considered all that was to come in their future. Perhaps it was a good sign that Pat had been able to retire easily. There was no erratic flickering behind his eyelids, like when he had a nightmare. He was lying perfectly on his back, as he did when he first fell asleep. Achilles wondered for a moment if it might not be best that he disappears now.

He shook his head, trying to clear his mind—he'd had too much to drink. Patroclus loved him.

But... Dio had said that he should take his death into his own hands. If Patroclus could make it through one night now, when he had a vague idea of Achilles' whereabouts, surely he would be better in the long run, versus at deployment when Achilles could be anywhere in the world.

Achilles turned and stumbled back down the hall, swaying to avoid hitting his hip on the banister, and ducked into the spare bedroom. Dionysus' words replayed in his mind over again while he stood in the dark.

The floor began to spin. The air siphoned itself from his lungs, and he felt as if he might suffocate if he stayed in place for a moment longer. His eyes found the window, and he ran to it as the walls closed in around him.

Achilles fumbled with the lock, letting out a frustrated groan, and finally tore the window open. He braced a foot on the ledge and looked out. The ground two stories below wavered in his vision, and he swallowed, turning to the roof. He braced a hand on either side of the frame and found a foothold before he began to climb.

The bricks that made up the side of the house were beginning to slick with morning dew, and he grabbed on to the gutter so he wouldn't fall.

"I'm too old for this," he muttered to himself as he heaved his body onto the garage roof.

It was slanted, but at a lower degree than the rest of the house, so he could stand without feeling as if he might fall.

He took a deep breath, letting his lungs expand completely, and looked to the stars. He searched the sky intently, as if he might see Thetis among the specks of light in whatever realm she was hiding in.

"Why did you do this to me, Mother?" he whispered.

A breeze tousled his hair, and he looked up to see a thunderhead rolling in. Raindrops began to fall onto his neighbor's house, and he climbed higher onto his roof before the downpour began over his own.

"Have you come to taunt me?" he called out.

As he glared at a particularly dark cloud, a flood of water burst free from the sky and wove down in a ribbon to gather in front of him before solidifying into the form of his mother.

Before he could say anything, she reached a fair hand out and stroked his cheek. Her large eyes looked sad, and she frowned as she stepped back.

"Why are you up here, Achilles?" she asked.

"Why did you curse me, Thetis?" he retorted.

She scoffed and backed up a step. "I did no such thing. I gave you the opportunity for greatness."

Achilles folded his arms, which threw his balance, and he steadied himself before jutting out his chin. "You bestowed a fate worse than mortal death on an infant that owed you nothing. Now I must pay the price for your sins."

"I granted you immortality and ensured a legacy for our family." She began to raise her voice, and water splashed at her feet.

"I never asked for this, Mother. I do not wish to leave a legacy. I do not want to leave my husband." Achilles choked on his words. "You've cursed my family to a life of misery and me to a horrible death. And in the event I don't want either option from this prophecy you bestowed, I'm not even sure if I can choose how I go. I don't want to run from death if I don't fall to heroism."

Rage stormed behind her eyes as she glared at him. "You're immortal, not invincible. Everyone has a weakness. That was the whole problem to begin with and why I tried to protect you from the worst parts of it."

Achilles froze. "I could have a way out."

"No. You have a responsibility. The Fates wove the thread of your life with greatness. Your future is to die in glory," she cried.

"I don't care to be great!" He raised his voice to match her desperation and stepped to the peak of the roof.

"It is your destiny!" she yelled.

"The destiny you chose!" Achilles yelled back. "I should have been mortal, allowed to live life as I chose, but you angered the Fates. You forced their hand."

She narrowed her eyes at him and backed farther away, letting her legs shift into their oceanic form. The wind and rain picked up around them and began to beat against the shingles. Achilles tried to take a step toward her but slipped and let out a hiss of pain.

"I was promised a son that would bring me recognition throughout the realms, that would be greater than his father," Thetis snapped, raising her hands toward Achilles.

"Maybe it's time to look to another child. I'm tired. I never asked for this."

Thetis spun up fully into a torrent, sending stinging saltwater flying for Achilles' face, and rose into the sky. The rain poured harder as she disappeared, and he was left to grip the roof, blinking droplets from his eyes.

He moved to walk across the peak again and was stopped by pain shooting up his leg. He lifted his foot to see that it had caught on a nail, and blood was leaking from the wound. He grimaced and crouched to sit, cradling his bare foot in one hand and using the other to brace himself so he didn't slide down the tiles.

He'd never seen himself bleed before, never seen his skin broken or bruised at all. Was this the weakness Thetis spoke of? Or had she done something?

He watched as the trickle of red was washed away with the rain. Maybe now was the perfect time to put Dionysus' advice into action. He looked over the edge of the roof, at the concrete pad of the driveway. Surely a fall from this height would cause him enough damage.

But what if it was a fluke? He might be left explaining how he fell, and recovered unharmed, to a neighbor that saw him. He'd accomplished more impressive feats before.

Achilles braced his hands against the rough shingles and stood, curling his toes to keep his balance while he paced along the length of the house and considered his options.

"Achilles!" Patroclus' voice cracked through the air.

He nearly lost his balance as he threw a hand to his chest, covering his stuttering heart. He looked down and blinked. Patroclus stood next to his car in a housecoat that appeared to have been tied hastily at the waist. He was staring with wide eyes up at Achilles, holding a hand above his eyes to shield himself from the rain. Achilles opened his mouth to call back, then closed it, unsure of what to say.

"What are you doing up there? Come down!"

"I don't want to," Achilles finally called back.

Patroclus groaned and stepped closer. "Is this about the summons? We'll find a way."

Achilles spread his arms and slid a little on the wet slate. He threw a hand out and grabbed a loose wire anchored to the chimney before looking down again. "What if this is the way? What if the only way to control my fate is to go on my own."

"What are you talking about? You can just decline." Patroclus' eyes widened.

Achilles shook his head. "You don't understand. It's not that simple."

"You're scaring me, Achilles. We can talk through this."

"She visited me, Patroclus. She told me that it's my only path, to bring her greatness. But I don't want it." His voice was hoarse as he spoke. "I don't want to leave you alone, but I can't run from the unknown, so I want to do it my way. I'm terrified. I'm not great, I'm weak."

Patroclus moved until he was nearly under the gutter, and Achilles saw that his curls were soaked through and plastered to his forehead. He wore his shoes with the heels pressed in, as if he'd slid into them in a rush.

"Listen to me. Whatever she said is wrong. Whatever you thought while you drank is wrong. I'm here and I'm not going anywhere. No matter what path we take, there will be fear. You have the capacity for greatness, even without death. You've always wanted it."

"I'm not drunk," Achilles returned.

"You've stumbled a few times since I came out here, even for someone standing on a house."

Achilles looked at his husband and tightened his grip on the cord, inching closer to it and crouching as he spoke. Thoughts whirled through his mind quickly as he considered. He heard Dionysus in his head, and Thetis. The shadows closed in around his mind, and he squeezed his eyes shut, trying to shake their words away. He could choose his fate. He could die now. But he was destined for greatness. He was worthless aside from the purpose chosen for him.

"Get off the roof, Achilles. I need you," Patroclus called.

Achilles was jerked from the onslaught of voices by the sound of metal clanging, and he looked down to see that Patroclus had opened the garage. He disappeared from view.

Achilles looked up to the sky, where the rain still poured down, before more banging sounds drew his attention back down to where his husband leaned a ladder against the gutter and held the base in place.

"Come down," he said in a soft voice.

Achilles took a deep breath before nodding. He stood, wobbling slightly, and inched toward the ladder. When he reached the top rung, he finally released the wire that had been holding him in place and climbed down one step at a time. Patroclus held it steady.

When he reached the ground, Patroclus gripped his shoulders and looked into his eyes.

"You scared the lights out of me. Don't ever do that again," he demanded.

Achilles nodded before Patroclus pulled him into an embrace, pressing his lips to Achilles' desperately. His body shuddered with a dry sob, and tears pricked Achilles' eyes.

Achilles pulled away after a moment, and they walked into the house together.

As they settled into bed, he held Patroclus' hand.

"I'll go in the morning and tell the office I won't deploy. There has to be a way out, and if not, I'll face a trial later."

Patroclus nodded against his shoulder. "One year in jail is better than ten overseas. We'll find ways to work around this."

The last thing Achilles thought before sleep took him was of the wound on his foot, and how it was beginning to throb painfully.

"Achilles? Achilles, wake up." Patroclus' voice was soft but urgent.

He opened his eyes and air-hissed through his teeth at the blinding light that assaulted them. He blinked rapidly to try and clear his vision, and pain thumped in the back of his head. He moaned as his husband's hand pressed into his chest.

"You've got to get going, the office will open soon."

"Mhm, okay, I'm up," Achilles muttered, half closing his eyes and falling back onto his pillow.

He felt the bed move next to him, and it was only a few moments later that he heard Patroclus turn on the shower before walking downstairs. He swore and rolled to face away from the window so he could gather his bearings and climb out of bed.

Every part of his body hurt and felt dry. He smacked his mouth a few times as he stepped under the hot water. The steady beat from the showerhead did little to ease the soreness in his muscles, and by the time he dressed, he still couldn't clear the caked feeling in his eyes.

He took the stairs slowly, feeling as if he might fall at any moment. Patroclus was already sitting at the table with a cup of coffee.

"Are you going to join me?" he asked.

Achilles paused for a moment before shaking his head. "I think it's best if I just get it over with, don't you?"

His husband nodded and gave him a small smile. "The sooner it happens, the sooner we can move on with our lives. Do you want me to go with you?"

"Don't you have work today?" Achilles asked.

"Yes, but I could always take a sick day," offered Patroclus.

Achilles shook his head. Everything felt slow and groggy as he kissed Patroclus goodbye.

The driveway wavered in his vision as he backed out, and he wondered if he should have taken up the offer for coffee, or company, but chided himself. He was on a mission to secure their future, and that was the most important thing. He'd be home soon anyway, and they'd be able to have lunch together.

He took the same route as the night before, and as he turned around a bend before entering the city, he remembered where he was and watched out his window.

On the left, he passed an empty parking lot, and a building sat near the back of it. A nerve in his jaw twitched as he looked for a neon sign, or heavy oak doors, and saw none. The windows were blacked out, and there were no identifying features about what should have been the bar that he drank at.

He gripped the wheel tight and continued driving, taking the turns toward downtown, where the secretary's office would be. As he drove, a strange sensation settled over his body. His stomach turned, and he began to feel anxious.

He briefly wondered if this was the right decision, then nodded firmly to himself. It had to be.

The prickling on the back of his neck continued as he turned a corner, and he noticed a woman through his right window walking down the sidewalk. She waved a hand toward a trash can, and a moment later it went flying down an alleyway. The hair on his arms raised and he swallowed hard as the discomfort continued to spread through his body.

Surely that was a coincidence. He'd already run into one god aside from his mother in the last day. There couldn't be another walking around this city.

She flung a hand out the other way, and he blinked.

Achilles looked back to the road, trying to ignore her, and gasped as something flew toward him. Cream and pastry splattered across his window a second before a small child darted out in front of him. He jerked his steering wheel to the right to avoid the boy and slammed on the brake pedal. As the vehicle stuttered to keep up with his command, he lost control of the steering and felt the mechanism begin to wobble.

He tried to steady the wheel, to turn back to the road, and pressed his foot to the floor as hard as possible, but time slowed. The steering wheel gave out beneath his fingers, and the brakes squealed underneath him.

The car careened out of control and headed toward a light pole, and Achilles watched as a man sat, reading a newspaper on a bench next to it, unaware. He slammed a hand to the horn, still trying to yank the wheel in any other direction. The steering column rattled uselessly under the dash, and the tires protested.

He hit the fog line, and the man finally looked up. Achilles' body went rigid, and he slammed both feet down. Patroclus flashed through his mind. He wished he'd stayed home, or left the house a little later. He wondered why this happened at this moment, and to him.

Just before the hood of Achilles' car made contact with the light pole, the man leaped out of the way. Achilles' scream filled his own ears as he felt every point of contact through the crash. His seatbelt yanked tightly against his waist. His head slammed hard against the metal wheel, then back against his leather seat. The front end of the car began to crunch, sending a ricochet back into his body, and the loud shattering and grinding of the car drowned out the sounds from his own mouth.

As his head met the glass of his window, he felt an excruciating pain through his leg. Something metal crunched through the bone at his foot, crushing his ankle and piercing through his calf. And as Achilles hit his head, the world went black.

Guide to The Five Realms

Aether – A Primordial Deity; often referred to as creation or the first point of creation; the spark of all life

Achilles – Immortal; Child of Thetis (Nereid)

Apate – Titan/higher God of Deception, often mistaken for a minor god, many forget Apate. He is one of the only higher gods descended from two Primordials – Nyx and Erebus

Aphrodite – Goddess of Love; Wife to Ares

Apollo – God of the Sun, primarily; Father of Asclepius

Asclepius – Demigod of Medicine; Child of Apollo and Coronis (Naiad)

Ares – God of the Spirit of Battle; often Zeus' right-hand man; Husband to Aphrodite

Artemis – Goddess of the Wild; Leader of The Hunters, a group of warriors who have chosen the pack as family

Athena – Goddess of Wisdom

Aurae – Nymphs of the sky; they can control the weather

Centaur – A race of Olympian with the lower half like a horse, some might have wings like a Pegasi, and the top half of a Mortal. Some Centaurs have extra arms or eyes like the Giants, as they were one of the first of the Titan races to be created and experimented with

Chaos – A Primordial Deity; the first creator and where Aether was born, holder of the gates of Tartarus (visit www.abdanielsannachi.com/extras for the universe origin story)

Cyclops – A race of Olympian that look like the Mortals in all ways but have elongated bodies and a single, or no, eye. They have an adept gift of intuition and were originally planned to be Oracles

Deimos – God of Terror; Child of Ares and Aphrodite

Demeter – Goddess of Agriculture

Demigod – Biological child of a god and either nymph, monster, or Mortal

Dionysus – Demigod of Pleasure

Drachma – The coin offered in worship to the gods; one must be cremated with a Drachma to pay for passage to Underworld

God – Creation of the Titans

Gryphon – A creature that was created to guard the underworld, with the body of a lion, wings, and the head of a hawk. Poseidon stole them from Hades' guard and experimented in combining them with Mortals until they could shift forms

Earth/Mortal Realm – The world on which Mortals live; magically tied to Olympus

Eris – Titan/higher Goddess of Chaos or Discord; created by Chaos, she holds the raw power of the Primordial Chaos, and could be just as powerful, but struggles to control it

Euthenia – Demigod; Child of Hephaestus

Fates – The three sisters that craft the threads of mortal life; Lachesis, Clotho, and Atropos. Clotho spins the yarns, Lachesis sorts the threads and decides when to snip them, and Atropos weaves the cloth of fate

Hades – God of the Sky or Thunder; Ruler of Underworld

Harpyai – A warrior race of Olympian created with beauty meant to distract; they have massive wings with colorful feathers of blades, and a beak that can snap bone

Hecate – Titan/higher Goddess of Gateways and Magic, primarily; one of the few gods descended genetically from the Titans Coeus and Crius and the God Zeus

Hephaestus – God of Craft

Hera – Goddess of Marriage, primarily; Wife to Zeus

Hermes – Titan/higher God of Travel, primarily; one of the few gods descended genetically from a line of Titans

Hestia – Goddess of the Hearth and Keeper of Olympus

Hypnos – A Primordial Deity; known as the God of Sleep

Ichor – The ethereal fluid that runs through gods' veins

Irohcin – A mix of ichor and blood, a term coined by the old gods

Myrmidon – Nymphs of the underground; they are insect related and only answer to Zeus

Napaea – Nymphs of the valley; they control flora and minor water life

Nephelai – Nymphs of the clouds; related to Aurae, they control clouds, help direct storms, and summon rain

Nereid – Nymphs of the sea; they preside over the oceans and are wards of Poseidon's

Nymph – A race of Olympian with many branches of power from woodland to mountain to ocean divinities that all control aspects of Olympus

Oceanid – Nymphs of the freshwater; they preside over the lakes and are related to Nereids

Olympus – Refers to both the full realm of Olympus and the city of Olympus (also sometimes called "The Golden City")

Olympian – Any being that was created in or born on Olympus, or shares genetic material with another Olympian and could survive living in Olympus; i.e., Gods, Demigods, Oceanids, Centaurs, Harpyai, etc.

Oracle – Mortal or Olympian chosen to channel prophecy

Pegasi – A warrior race of Olympian

Poseidon – God of the Sea; also known as "Don"

Priapus – Demigod of Gardens; Child of Dionysus

Primordial – The original beings; creators of all realms

Tartarus – A prison created by Chaos for beings of any other realm

Titan – Creation of the Primordials

Titan God – Biological descendant of Titans; normally child of two Titans but sometimes a descendant of a line of Titans

Underworld – The realm of death

Zeus – God of the Sky or Thunder; King of Gods

About the Author

Ari is a trans author and editor from Oregon. After having his first novel published while living in Australia—a true crime memoir—he quickly dove into writing fantasy. He  spends his free time reading, listening to mythology podcasts, and playing D&D. Follow him on Instagram, Facebook, or TikTok @darkmythauthor to stay up to date. To learn more about him and his books, visit:

www.abdanielsannachi.com

www.ingramcontent.com/pod-product-compliance
Lightning Source LLC
Chambersburg PA
CBHW030811190726
48285CB00003B/1129